Goodnight Tennis
Bedtime tennis story for kids

Goodnight tennis. Bedtime tennis story for kids.
Cooolz Ltd., 2023. 32 pages, illustrated.

ISBN 9798386289102
Publisher   Cooolz Ltd.
Author   Janina Spruza

Dear friends!
Settle down comfortably and listen to this story about the amazing things that happened to two kids just like you who found themselves in a magical city of tennis!

There once was a brother and sister whose bedroom window overlooked some tennis courts. Each night before going to bed, the children would look out the window and wonder:

"Why are there always so many people
down there, and what are they doing?
What is going on? It looks like fun!"

One evening, while the children were playing with their toys, a star flew into their room through the window:

"Hello, children! My name is Ace. Every night, I see you looking out the window at the courts. So, tonight I would like to invite you to the marvelous tennis city! But first, please accept these tennis rackets as a gift from me."

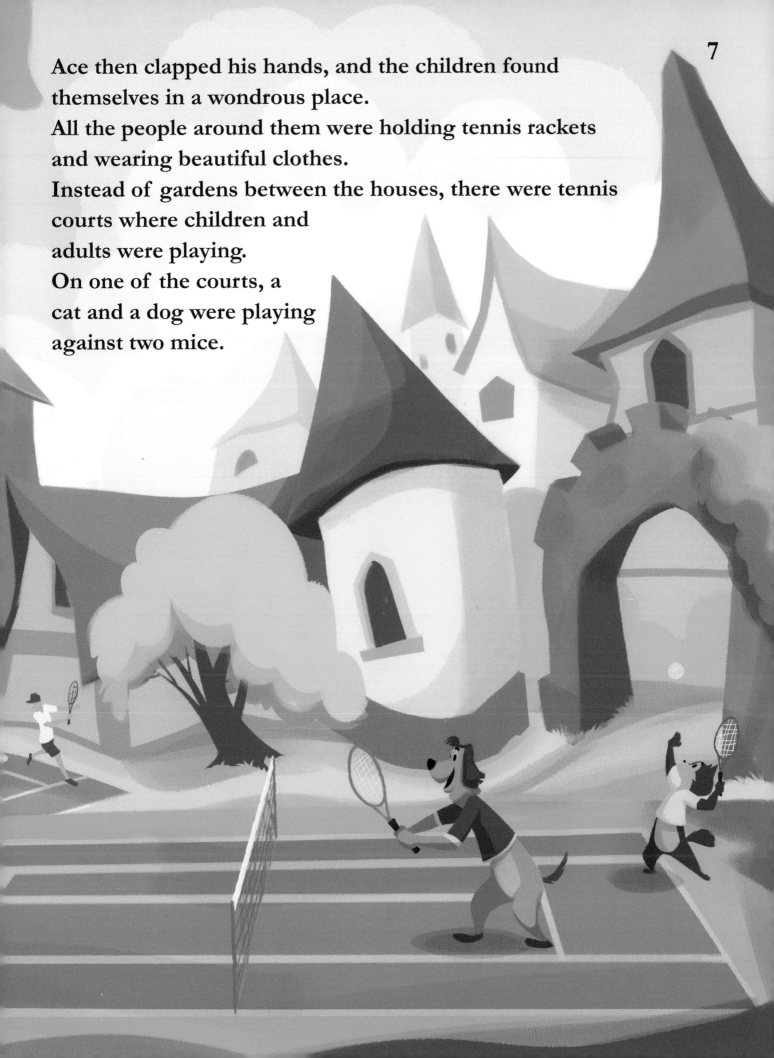

Ace then clapped his hands, and the children found
themselves in a wondrous place.
All the people around them were holding tennis rackets
and wearing beautiful clothes.
Instead of gardens between the houses, there were tennis
courts where children and
adults were playing.
On one of the courts, a
cat and a dog were playing
against two mice.

The brother and sister followed Ace to an open court.
"Let's get to know tennis a little better," said Ace.
"I will be your first coach.
Oh, I forgot to properly introduce myself. You already know
my name, but you don't know who I am yet. I am Ace,
named after everyone's favorite tennis stroke."

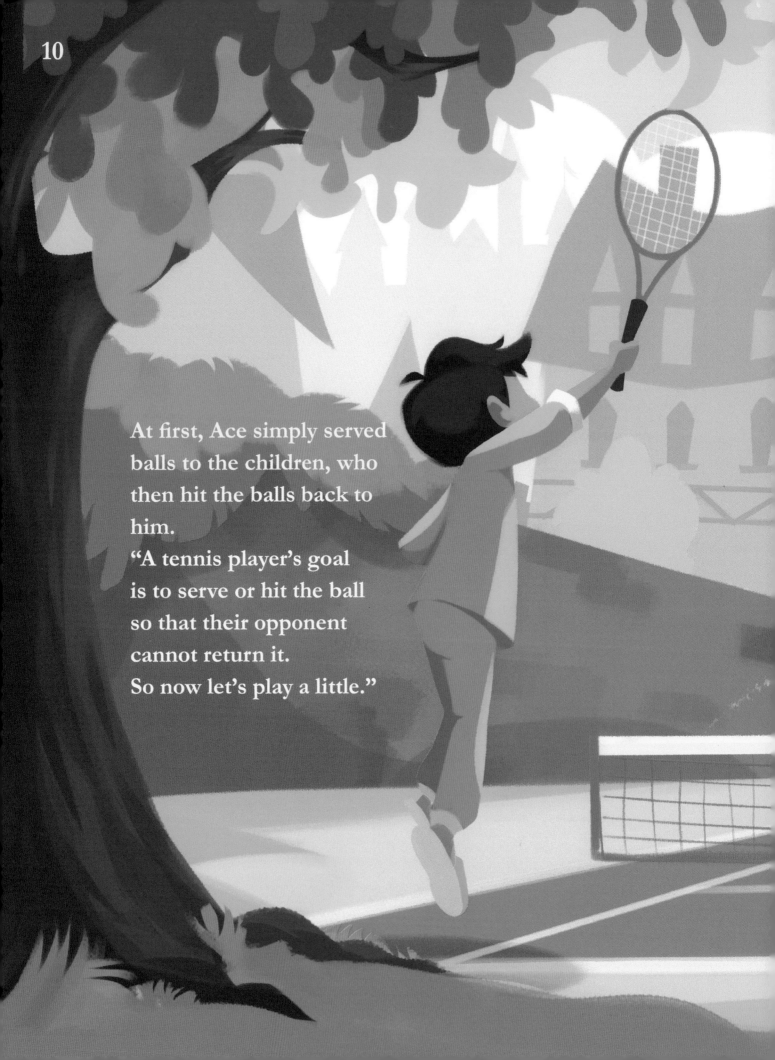

At first, Ace simply served balls to the children, who then hit the balls back to him.
"A tennis player's goal is to serve or hit the ball so that their opponent cannot return it.
So now let's play a little."

The boy served the ball so well that Ace was barely able to hit it back. And when Ace served, the sister was easily able to return the ball.

Ace cheered. "Wow! You are the most talented children I've ever seen! We're not going to worry about the rules of the game today. Instead, let's go into the Magic Room."

The children suddenly found themselves at the entrance to an unusual building. An enchanting light streamed from a small window, and on the front door hung a lock and a piece of paper. The note said, "To open this door, you must find a 'key' made up of four parts. Each part is a title that is located in one of four countries. And we will visit each of the countries, because tonight is a magical night."

Ace clapped his hands, and the children found themselves in a super-modern city with shiny skyscrapers. On the shoreline stood a fabulous building that looked like a giant seashell.

"We are in Sydney, the capital city of Australia. And this gorgeous building is the Sydney Opera House."

Suddenly, in the sky directly above the Opera House, the words "Australian Open" appeared in huge, bright letters for a few seconds.

"Got that memorized? Now let's go find the next part!" said Ace, and he clapped his hands again.

Australian Open

Rolland Garros

The children instantly found themselves in another beautiful city with an amazing tower.
"This is the capital of France, Paris. And that is the famous Eiffel Tower."

Suddenly, in the sky behind the Eiffel Tower, in enormous, bright letters, the words "Rolland Garros" appeared for just a moment.

"There it is. Will you remember that, kids? Okay. Let's go get the next part!"

What an incredible city! Double-decker buses were driving through the streets, and there were red telephone booths here and there on the sidewalks.

"Now we are in London, the capital of England. There are a huge number of interesting places and buildings here. This tower with its clock, for example, is the world famous Big Ben. But look and see what's in the sky!"

And for just the blink of an eye, huge letters spelling
"Wimbledon" lit up over Big Ben.
"That's the third part of the key. Hurry! There's no time to lose!
Let's find the fourth part, get into the Magic Room, and go to
bed on time."
Ace clapped his hands.

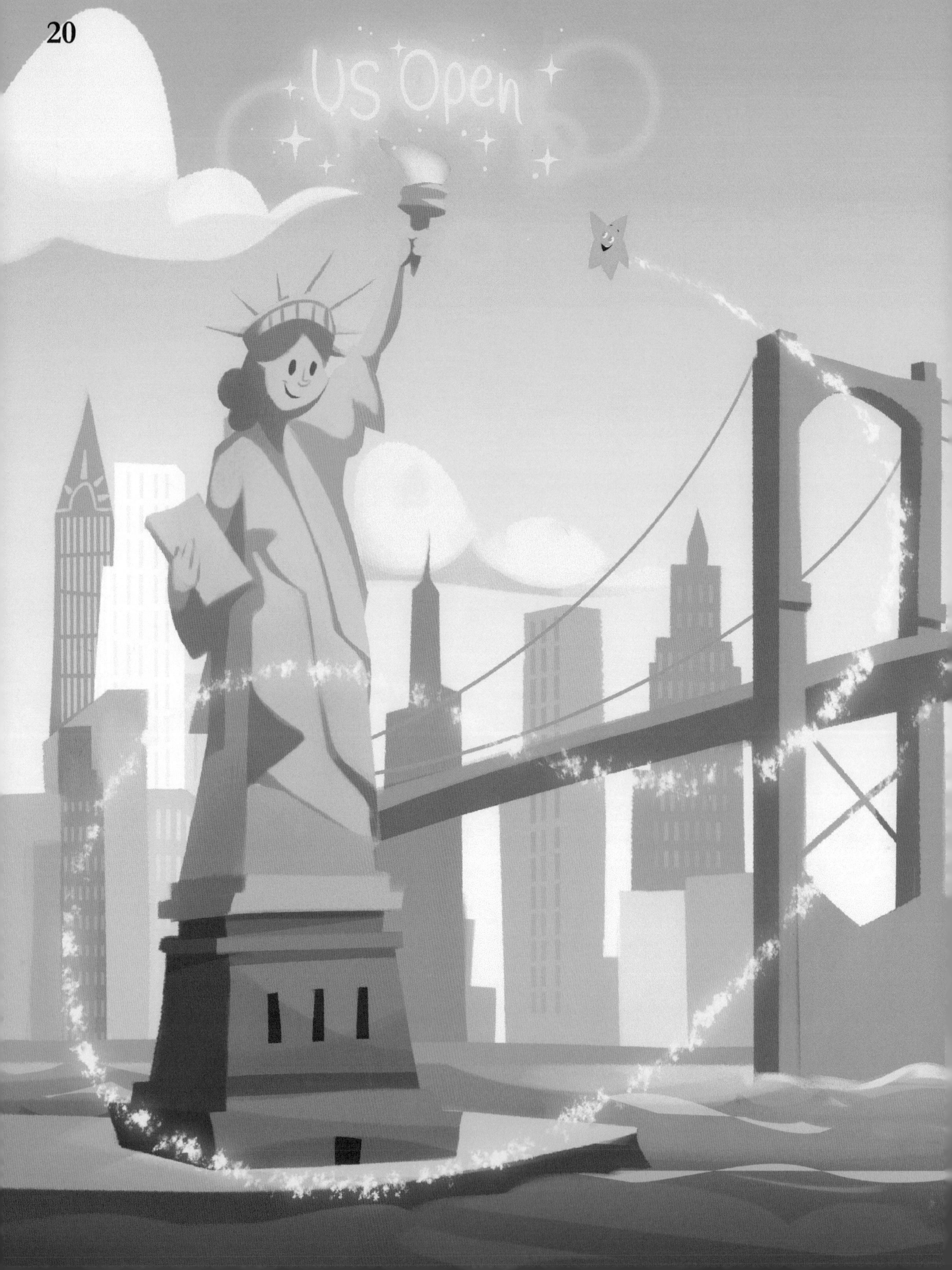
US Open

The children recognized this statue immediately. They have seen this symbol of the United States many times: the Statue of Liberty in New York.

"Well now. Our last piece of the key should be here somewhere." Suddenly, the Statue of Liberty smiled, and appearing from her torch came the words "US Open."

"Hooray! We found all four parts!"

In a blink, the children were once again in front of the magic door.

They wrote all four titles on the piece of paper… and the magic door opened!

The whole room glowed with many colors. In the middle of the room was a pedestal on which stood an iridescent, transparent object shaped like a goblet.

"This is the most coveted trophy in tennis – the Grand Slam. In reality, it's just a title, but everyone wants it.
However, a player can only win the title if they have won the Olympic Games and all four tournaments whose names we collected around the world."

"We didn't have to search for the name of the Olympics, because the Games are held in a different country each time.
And now, it's time to go home. It's time for bed!"

Ace clapped his hands, and the children were one
again in their room.

"Knock-knock-knock." Their mother and father
glanced into the room.

"Daddy! Mommy!
We just had the greatest adventure of our lives! We saw incredible things!
Please promise us that we can go play tennis tomorrow.
It's the best game! We will play tennis all together as a family, and then you'll be in the fairytale, too!"

The brother and sister crawled under their covers, hugged their tennis rackets, and fell sound asleep.

All night long, they each had the same dream of playing tennis and winning the Grand Slam.

"Good night, dear tennis!"
"Good night, dear friend Ace!"
"Good night, dear Grand Slam!"

Goodnight tennis.
Bedtime tennis story for kids.
Cooolz Ltd., 2023. 32 pages, illustrated.

Author Janina Spruza

ISBN 9798386289102

Printed in Great Britain
by Amazon

24471342R00018